To

........................,

Merry Christmas!
Love,

....

'Twas the night before Christmas,
when all through the house,
Not a creature was stirring,
not even a mouse;
Your stocking was hung
by the chimney with care,
In hope that St. Nicholas soon would be there.

....................................., you were nestled all snug in your bed,
While visions of candy canes danced in your head.
And Mom in her kerchief, and Dad in his cap,
Had just settled down for a long winter's nap.

When out on the street
there arose such a clatter,
You sprang from your bed
to see what was the matter.
Away to the window
you flew like a flash,
Tore open the curtains,
threw open the latch.

The moon on the blanket
of new-fallen snow,
Shone bright as midday
on the objects below—

When, what to your
wondering eyes should appear,
But a miniature sleigh
and eight tiny reindeer.

With a little old driver,
so lively and quick,
.... knew in a moment
it must be St. Nick.
More rapid than eagles
his reindeer they came,
And he whistled, and shouted,
and called them by name:

Merry
Christmas

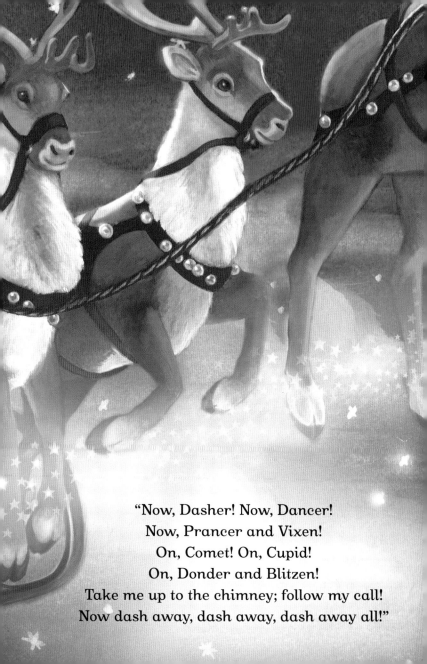

"Now, Dasher! Now, Dancer!
Now, Prancer and Vixen!
On, Comet! On, Cupid!
On, Donder and Blitzen!
Take me up to the chimney; follow my call!
Now dash away, dash away, dash away all!"

And then, in a twinkling,
you heard on the roof
The prancing and pawing
of each little hoof.

As you pulled in your head
and were turning around,
Down the chimney
St. Nicholas came with a bound.

He was dressed all in fur,
from his head to his foot,
And his clothes were all tarnished
with ashes and soot.
A bundle of toys he had
flung on his back,
And he looked like a peddler
holding his pack.

Merry
Christmas

His eyes—how they twinkled!
His dimples—how merry!
His cheeks were like roses,
his nose like a cherry.
His droll little mouth
was drawn up like a bow,
And the beard on his chin was
as white as the snow.

Dear Santa,
I hope you enjoy
the sweet treats.
Love,

P.S. The carrots
are for your
furry friends.

A big sack of toys
he held tight in his fist,
And he glanced to find your name
on his Nice List.
He had a broad face
and a little round belly
That shook when he laughed,
like a bowl full of jelly.

NICE LIST

Steven
Lola
Marcus
Elana

He was chubby and plump,
a right jolly old elf,
And you laughed when you saw him,
in spite of yourself.

St. Nick winked an eye
and tilted his head
Letting you know
you had nothing to dread.

He spoke not a word,
but went straight to his work,
And filled up your stocking,
then turned with a jerk.

And tapping his finger at the side of his nose,
And giving a nod, up the chimney he rose.

He sprang to his sleigh, to his team gave a whistle,
And away they all flew like the down of a thistle.
But St. Nicholas exclaimed, as he drove out of sight—

....,
draw all your favorite
Christmas presents from Santa.

Adapted from the poem by Clement C. Moore
Illustrated by Lisa Alderson
Designed by Jane Gollner

Published by Put Me In The Story,
a publication of Sourcebooks, Inc.
P.O. Box 4410, Naperville, Illinois 60567-4410
(630) 536-1104
www.putmeinthestory.com

Date of Production: June 2021
Run Number: 5022128
Printed and bound in Italy (LG)
10 9 8 7 6 5 4 3

MIX
Paper from
responsible sources
FSC® C023419
www.fsc.org

put me
in the story®
Bestselling books starring your child!
www.putmeinthestory.com